About the Book

Waza was a pure white camel. She was part of the army's Camel Brigade. Dirtyshirt Dan hated camels, especially Waza. He hated them because he was the chief mule driver and the camels, especially Waza, did a better job than his mules.

Dirtyshirt Dan was determined to disgrace Waza. But every time he tried, something unexpected happened, and Waza always won!

In the 1850's two shiploads of camels were brought to Texas to be used as pack animals on the trail to California. Eleanor Coerr has based her funny story on some of the hilarious reports that appeared in newspapers at the time.

Waza Wins at Windy Gulch

by Eleanor Coerr   illustrated by Janet McCaffery

A See and Read Storybook

G. P. Putnam's Sons   New York

Text copyright © 1977 by Eleanor Coerr
Illustrations copyright © 1977 by Janet McCaffery
All rights reserved. Published
simultaneously in Canada by
Longman Canada Limited, Toronto.
PRINTED IN THE UNITED STATES OF AMERICA
06209
Library of Congress Cataloging in Publication Data
Coerr, Eleanor.
Waza wins at Windy Gulch.
(See and read storybooks)
SUMMARY: A camel that was brought to the United
States to be used as a pack animal causes a stir when
it foils a bank robbery.
[1. Camels—Fiction. 2. The West—History—1848-
1950—Fiction] I. McCaffery, Janet. II. Title.
PZ7.C6567Was [Fic] 76-21224
ISBN 0-399-20564-0 ISBN 0-399-61053-7 lib. bdg.

Waza Wins at Windy Gulch

Jan 22/83.

For Michael,

Love

Eleanor Coerr.

How the Camels Got Here

In the 1850s, Jefferson Davis, Secretary of War, had two shiploads of camels brought to Texas. Most of them came from Egypt, Turkey, and Saudi Arabia. Hi Jolly and other camel drivers came, too.

Lieutenant Beale used the camels as pack animals on the trail to California. Many funny things happened to the Camel Brigade in the West. Some were reported in newspapers. Others were told around campfires. A few of the stories are in this book.

This is Waza.
She was part of the Camel Brigade.
Hi Jolly was the chief camel driver.
He loved all his camels. But he
especially loved pure-white Waza.

This is Dirtyshirt Dan.
He was the chief mule driver.
And he hated all camels.
But he especially hated Waza.
Once she came too close to
his mules.
"Git away from my animals!" he
snarled. "You smelly, useless
critter!"

Hi Jolly stroked Waza's neck.
"Don't listen to him," he said
softly. "We know that camels
are important."
And they were.
Lieutenant Beale had brought
two shiploads of camels and
some camel drivers to the
United States. The animals carried
supplies for the Army.

Every morning Hi Jolly and his
men loaded the camels. Then
they started out. Far behind
came Dirtyshirt Dan and his mules.
Soon everyone could see that
camels worked better than mules.
They could carry bigger loads.
They could go longer without water.
And they could find their own
food in the desert.
That is why the trouble began.

Dirtyshirt Dan was jealous.
He didn't want the camels to
outshine his mules. No, sir!
"We must think of a way to make
those camels look bad," he told
his men. "Or the Army won't need
our mules anymore."
He thought and thought.
Then something happened to make
him really angry.
After a long, dry day the
brigade camped near a waterhole.
The thirsty mules made a wild
dash for the water.
Dirtyshirt Dan waved his arms
at them and yelled, "Stop!"
But the mules kept on going
and drank so much water they
got sick.

The camels were smarter than that.
They didn't drink one drop until
Hi Jolly sang their water song.

"Terrah!"

Then they drank with throaty gurgles.
"Come and see!" Dirtyshirt Dan called
to his men. "These stupid, puddin'footed
beasts don't know enough to drink
without being told."
"Camels aren't stupid," Hi Jolly
said. "They just know my songs."
"Singing to camels!" shouted
Dirtyshirt Dan. "Crazy as popcorn
on a hot stove!"

The mule drivers laughed.
Waza looked down her long nose
at the chief mule driver. Then
she spat right in his eye.
Dirtyshirt Dan let out a yell.
"I'll get you, you low-down,
four-footed hoodoo!"

Waza bared her big yellow teeth
at him. The camel drivers laughed.
Then and there Dirtyshirt Dan made
up his mind to get rid of the camels.
"I'll see those loop-necked monsters
shipped back where they came from,"
he boasted, "or I'm not Dirtyshirt Dan!"

He secretly learned some of the camel songs.
Then he waited for his chance.
Finally, it came.
A scout told Lieutenant Beale that a herd
of cattle was camped nearby.
"We'll stay far away," Lieutenant Beale said,
"so there won't be any trouble."
Dirtyshirt Dan laughed nastily.
He knew exactly what kind of trouble
camels could make for a herd of cattle.
Late that night he crept up to Waza.
She was ready to growl at him until
he rubbed her neck. How she loved that!
She let Dirtyshirt Dan take off the
hobbles and lead her quietly away.

Soon they stopped. Dirtyshirt Dan
tapped Waza's knees with a stick.
He sang the kneeling song,
"Eteee! Eteee! Eteee!"
Waza groaned, "HARRUUUMPH!"
as she knelt down.
Dirtyshirt Dan climbed onto her back.
Waza grumbled, "ANNNWHURRR!"
and started to stand up.
First, she reared up on her front legs.
Dirtyshirt Dan almost fell off backward.

Then up came her hind legs.
Dirtyshirt Dan almost flew forward
over her head.
"What a dangfool way to stand up!"
he muttered.

He hung on as Waza swayed across the plains. Before long he was pale.
And wobbly. And seasick.
He was so sick he had to get off.

Waza kept on going right toward
the cattle. A breeze carried the
whiffy camel smell to the herd.
One steer lifted his head, sniffed
and rumbled, "O-OOOOM?"
He got the full thick smell.
It was strange and scary.
So he roared a warning.
"BAAAWR-R-R!"

In a flash the herd was bawling and
stampeding. The frightened animals
knocked over the chuck wagon.
Cowboys jumped out of their bedrolls
and tried to find their horses.

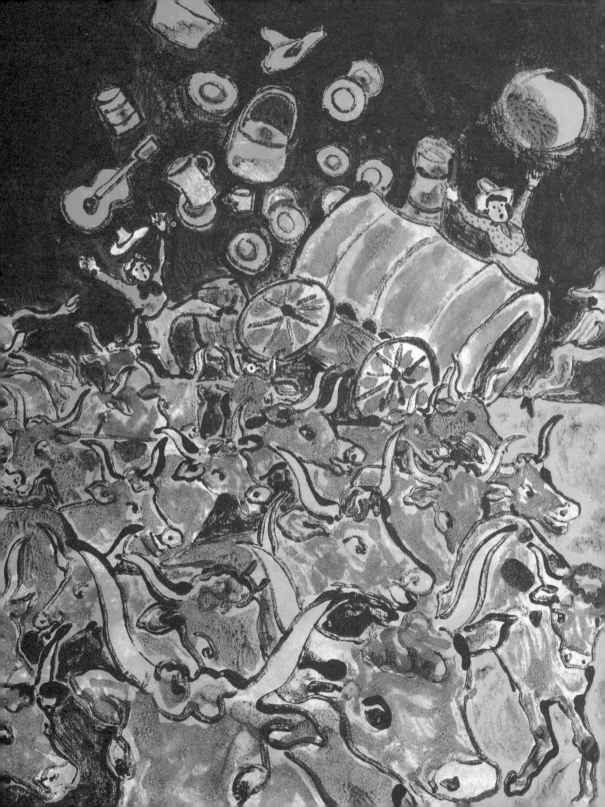

All that noise made Waza tired.
She yawned and knelt down for a nap.
When the trail boss saw
Waza in the morning, he knew
what had happened.
He galloped to the Camel Brigade.
The whole camp could hear him yelling
at Lieutenant Beale.
"Yippee!" shouted the mule drivers.
"That will be the end of camels!"
Dirtyshirt Dan stuck out his chest.
"I told you I could do it," he said
proudly. "Now the brutes will be
shipped home."

But no.
Instead, Lieutenant Beale ordered the mule
drivers to round up the lost cattle.
For days Dirtyshirt Dan was as cross
as a teased snake. He waited for
another chance.

One evening the Camel Brigade camped
near the town of Windy Gulch.
The next day Lieutenant Beale and Hi Jolly
put on their best clothes and
went into town.

"This is it," Dirtyshirt Dan told his men. "I'll get that smart-aleck camel into REAL trouble."

He knew what a camel could do to a town!

Once again, Dirtyshirt Dan took Waza away from camp. This time he rode on his mule and led Waza with a long rope.

Near town he let her go free. "Spread your smell around Windy Gulch," he shouted. "You rubber-necked stack of bones!"

Then Dirtyshirt Dan rode fast into town. He wanted to be there when the fun began.

It was a quiet afternoon in Windy Gulch. That is, until Waza ambled down Main Street.

Her strange shape and smell were
too much for the animals.
Pigs and dogs and chickens
scattered this way and that.

All the horses snorted and galloped
away.
Dirtyshirt Dan almost split his
sides laughing.
Waza stopped in front of Bearpaw
Smith's General Store.
The mule driver shouted, "Don't
stop now!" And he gave her an extra-
hard smack on the rear.
With an angry bellow, Waza jumped
onto the porch. She pushed the
posts over.
KER-SMASH!
The porch roof fell down.
"Ho! Ho! He-e-e!" roared Dirtyshirt Dan.
Suddenly he stopped laughing.
A piece of wood zonked him on the head.
He fell into the water trough.

When the dust settled, there stood
Waza in the middle of Main Street.
"Great snakes and centipedes!" yelled
Bearpaw Smith. "What's that?"
"Looks like a moose without antlers,"
someone said.

"It couldn't be," a little boy screamed, "but it is! A real-for-sure camel!"

Hi Jolly ran after Waza.

"Walloo! Walloo! Walloo!" he sang.
Waza heard her master's voice
and stopped in front of the bank.
Just then the door flew open.
Two bandits ran out. They had guns
and bags of money. They went for
their horses. But the horses were
gone. In their place stood one
huge white camel.
The bandits looked dazed.
The sheriff moved fast.
Before the bandits knew what had
happened, they were in jail.

When Dirtyshirt Dan came to, he
saw a crowd around Waza.
He thought the camel was in big trouble.

But something was wrong.
The crowd was cheering, "Hurray
for the camel! She saved the bank!"

Dirtyshirt Dan went closer.

When he heard what had happened, he tried to sneak away.

But Waza saw him. She gallumphed over to have her neck rubbed.

Dirtyshirt Dan glared at her.

"Git!" he hissed. "You bad luck beast!"

Waza only pushed her scrunchy mouth against his shoulder. Lieutenant Beale was surprised. "How wonderful that camels like you!" he said to Dirtyshirt Dan. "Because Hi Jolly needs another camel driver."

"Oh, no!" said Dirtyshirt Dan.

"Oh, yes!" said Lieutenant Beale.

Dirtyshirt Dan groaned. He knew the
men would laugh him out of camp.

So he got on his mule and hit the trail. And the Camel Brigade never saw him again.
He made sure of that.

What Happened to the Camels?

After about ten years, the United States government decided not to use camels anymore. Many were sold, and the rest set free in the deserts of the Southwest.

Waza lived to a ripe old age in the wilds of Arizona. Hi Jolly stayed in the United States. He died in 1902. You can still visit his grave in Quartzite, Arizona. It is marked by a tall stone pyramid with a metal camel on top.